ORSO
THE TROLL WHO COULDN'T SCARE

WRITTEN BY BRAD THIESSEN
AND
ILLUSTRATED BY JEREMY BALZER

cds
BOOKS

For Kyle
AND
For Kim

For information please address:

CDS Books
425 Madison Avenue
New York, NY 10017

ISBN: 1-59315-142-X

Orders, inquiries, and correspondence should be addressed to:

CDS Books
425 Madison Avenue
New York, NY 10017
(212) 223-2969 FAX (212) 223-1504

Design by Mulberry Tree Press

Printed in Singapore

10 9 8 7 6 5 4 3 2 1

ORSO the troll lived with his father in a cave under a bridge.

His father spent every day scaring people who tried to cross the bridge.

But Orso didn't like to scare people. Instead, he would go for walks in the hills, and climb trees.

Sometimes he would just look up at the sky and pretend the clouds were talking to him.

On the day that Orso turned eight years old, he felt a bit lonely.
"Dad, how come we don't have any friends?" he asked.
"Because we're trolls, and trolls don't have friends."

Later, as his father was tucking him into bed, Orso said, "I wish I had lots of friends. Or at least just one."

"Well, you've got me," his father replied.

Orso gave his father the biggest hug an eight-year-old can give.

"Stop it!" his father laughed. "That tickles!"

Orso didn't stop. Instead, he tickled all the harder. His father laughed a huge, rolling troll laugh that shook the ground for miles around.

The next morning, Orso's father told him it was time he learned how to scare people. They crouched under the bridge and waited. And waited. And waited.

After a while, Orso crept out to talk with his cloud friends. Today, though, they frowned at him. In the breeze that blew past, he heard them say, "What are you doing? Why would you scare people?"

A bit ashamed, Orso crawled back to sit with his father.

As it began to get dark, Orso's tummy felt empty.

"Can we go now?" he asked.

Orso heard the clip-clop of horses' feet, and the creaking of wagon wheels. As the sounds came closer and closer, his heart beat faster and faster.

Suddenly Orso's father leaped out and
growled his loudest and meanest troll growl.
By the time the last echo had died away, the
wagon and its people were gone.

"See, son?" said Orso's father. "Now that's
how you scare people!" But Orso wasn't there
either.

Orso's father found the young troll hiding in his bedroom.

"What's wrong, son?" he asked.

Orso didn't reply. He was still thinking of his father's frightening face back on the bridge.

"Scaring people is stupid," Orso said. "It's no fun at all."

"You're a troll, and trolls have to scare people," his father said. "We aren't good at anything else."

"What about construction?" His father held up his big, lumpy hands. "We can't hold a hammer."

"We could try farming," Orso said.
"We'd scare the animals," his father replied.

"We could be musicians," Orso
said, and began singing his favorite
song. But he had to admit that
trolls don't make very good singers,
either.

The next morning, Orso got up before it was light, and crept out the door.

It was a beautiful morning. The dew on the grass made his feet tingle. The morning breeze carried the scent of lilacs and pine trees. Frogs, bees, and birds filled the air with their good-morning songs.

From the top of the tallest tree in the forest, Orso saw his father look around a moment before slowly disappearing under the bridge.

As he climbed down the tree, Orso heard laughter, and saw a girl and boy playing below. He wished he could play with them.

But Orso was a troll and he knew what a troll was supposed to do.
"Aaargh! Roar!" yelled Orso in his best troll growl, as he leaped from the tree.
The boy looked a little scared, and ready to run away. But the girl laughed.
"Do that again," she said.

"I was trying to scare you," said Orso. "Only I'm not so good at it."
"No, you're not," said the girl. "But you're good at making me laugh."

All that day, Orso played with the girl, whose name was Lizzy, and the boy, whose name was Jacob. Before they knew it, the sun was setting.
"We've got to get home!" cried Lizzy. "Mom will be worried!"

As they reached the bridge near Orso's home, the troll and his friends saw a torch bobbing in the darkness and behind it, a man's worried face.
"Daddy!" cried Lizzy and Jacob.

Suddenly a huge, hairy creature jumped out from the darkness and let loose a roar that shook the bridge and filled the countryside.

"It's a troll!" cried the children's father. "I'm not scared of you, monster!"

Orso looked at his father, who was so kind and gentle with him but so rough and mean to everyone else. Then he looked at Lizzy and Jacob, and he knew what he had to do. He crept behind the children's father, reached out his hairy arms . . .

. . . and tickled him.

"There are two monsters!" the man shouted.

Lizzy laughed. "He's not a monster, Daddy. He's Orso."

"Yeah," said Jacob. "We've been playing together all day!"

"He looks like a troll!" gasped her father.

"I am," said Orso. "But not a scary troll. I'm a tickle troll!"

"What about the big one?" asked the children's father.

"Don't worry about me," sighed Orso's father. "Once people hear about my son, no one's going to be scared of us anymore. We'll have to find a new home, with new people to frighten."

"We can't leave," Orso cried out. "Jacob and Lizzy are my new friends!"

"Yeah," said Jacob. "We think Orso's the funnest troll ever!"

"He is?" Orso's father asked.

"Sure," said Lizzy. "I bet people would come from all over if they knew how much fun he is!"

From that day on, Orso and his father spent every morning walking in the hills, and climbing trees, and listening to the birds.

After lunch, they hid under the bridge and waited for people to come by so they could jump out and surprise them. Orso perfected the art of tickling. His father learned to tell jokes.

And at Orso's ninth birthday party, his father gave him a huge cake, enough to share with all their new friends.